This Book Belongs To:

_____

Dedications:

I dedicate this book first to my three beautiful children, Megan, Ryan, and Anna for their unconditional love, support, and encouragement in all of my endeavors. I also dedicate my work to Blessed Mother Teresa for sharing with the world her very prayerful, humble, and simple existence and providing for us a flawless example of what it means to truly appreciate the absolute value of every human being.

- Julie Anne Bisi

To OAPX Raphael, my nieces and nephews, and Grandma Hill.

- Amy Hill

Library of Congress Control Number:
2010915665
ISBN Number: 978-0-615-40372-4
Published in Latrobe, PA by Apollo Design Group, Inc.

The Lord doesn't see things the way you see them. People judge by outward appearance, but the Lord looks at the heart.

1 Samuel 16:7

Imagine.

 magine a house.

gigantic house perched on a hill at the edge of a very small town.

8

No swing set. No sandbox. No toys scattered on the lawn. Not even a single lonely cat prowling about in the shadows. Yet a stream of smoke constantly rose from the chimney of this enormous dwelling while only a single light ever glowed from deep within.

For years we stood and gazed at that mysterious house on the other side of the forbidden railroad tracks, as our imaginations ran wild with tales of evil lurking inside that decrepit old building.

espite our curiosity, we managed for a long time to come up with every excuse possible to avoid examining the house more closely. Yet somehow, at the end of our daily paper route, we always found ourselves walking slowly down Depot Street to catch one last glimpse.

ne Saturday, I got out of bed a little earlier than usual. Just as I finished my bowl of cereal, I heard the familiar rattle of two bicycles pedaling down Ridge Avenue as my cousins, Kevin and Kelli, arrived. Their normal look of excitement was replaced, however, with long worried expressions, for we had a very serious and dangerous mission awaiting us. The time had finally come for us to solve the mystery of the house on the hill.

I can still remember the smile on my mother's face as she bid us farewell that morning. She had no idea what danger awaited the three of us. What were we thinking?!?

We did not hop eagerly onto our bikes and ride off, as we usually did. Instead, we walked silently beside them, down Ridge Avenue toward our destiny. I looked back longingly at my mother and the place that held so many fond memories. I quietly said a private good-bye to my parents and each of my siblings. I tried to imagine the reaction of my family if we did not return home from our journey. Even though I was sure they would mourn our loss (except for my brother Eddy, of course), I was equally convinced that they would be so impressed with our bravery. Surely they would understand that we had a responsibility to keep our neighborhood safe. We knew that we should have shared our worries with someone but we were afraid they would tell us not to go.

Although we did not speak for quite some time, we were fully aware of each other's thoughts. At one point, I looked down and saw that our feet were moving in the same order at the same time. Surely a good sign...

n the first ten minutes of our journey, we found that we had traveled only two blocks. Although no one was ready to back out, Kelli was the first to attempt to prolong the inevitable.

"Uh, l-let's go get our p-papers first. We better d-deliver them to the stores b-before they get mad and c-call our p-parents." Thankful for the delay, we eagerly agreed.

22

s we moved in and out of the stores, our faces must have revealed the weight of our burden. Normally, we were happy and carefree, "a breath of fresh air," as we were often told. Our customers always seemed eager for our leisurely visits and stories from the week gone-by. However, on that day, our bodies must have told a different tale altogether. We were sullen and secretive; somber and silent. Many thought we were sick. Others inquired about the health of our family members. Doctor Hazlett even made us wait until he checked our temperature and blood pressure. Each of them, though, eventually accepted our response that nothing was wrong and unknowingly sent us off to face our final doom.

e finally arrived at our destination, unable to procrastinate any longer. Kevin, the bravest of all, climbed the rotted steps to set our plan in motion while Kelli and I cowered behind the safety of a nearby tree. His fingers rose slowly to the knocker dangling from the splintered door.

Much to our surprise, a very soft-spoken and gentle old woman appeared. No warts! No black dress! Not even a lousy broom! So much for danger!! We were completely speechless (a rare occurence) and, I must admit, rather disappointed.

After what seemed like an eternity of silence, Kevin finally muttered the only words that came to mind as our dream to become neighborhood superheroes vanished before our eyes, "Uh, uh, excuse me, ma'am, we deliver newspapers in this town and were wondering if you would like us to add you to our route."

"Not in the plan book, Kevin," I muttered under my breath, slightly irritated with the turn of events.

h, children, you have made my day," she responded with tears streaming down her cheeks. "Of course I would! You know, my husband and I bought this big, old house years ago. We both retired and, since it sits next to the railroad station, planned to make it into an inn for weary travelers. Unfortunately, my husband passed away before we could finish the work outside. Even though I have a beautiful home on the inside, people cannot get past the eerie feeling they get when they look at it from the street. I have not had a visitor in years and have never been able to serve a single customer. I am so excited that you knocked at my door. Can you believe some people actually think this house is haunted?"

"Nooooo!?!" we said in unison, our mouths gaping open.

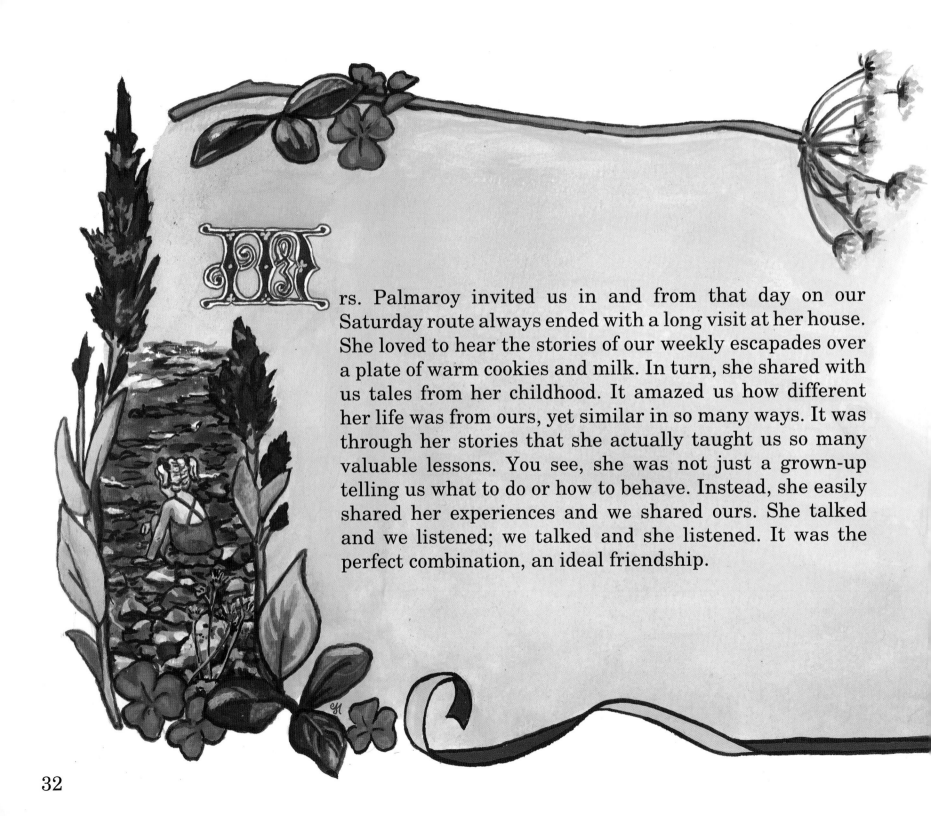

Mrs. Palmaroy invited us in and from that day on our Saturday route always ended with a long visit at her house. She loved to hear the stories of our weekly escapades over a plate of warm cookies and milk. In turn, she shared with us tales from her childhood. It amazed us how different her life was from ours, yet similar in so many ways. It was through her stories that she actually taught us so many valuable lessons. You see, she was not just a grown-up telling us what to do or how to behave. Instead, she easily shared her experiences and we shared ours. She talked and we listened; we talked and she listened. It was the perfect combination, an ideal friendship.

ver time, we recruited the help of family and friends in an effort to give the old house a new facelift. Unfortunately, timing is everything and even though her home took on a much more inviting look, the train station no longer brought enough travelers to our town to warrant the need for an inn. However, the four of us agreed that all was not a total loss. We understood that it was truly the creepy exterior (and of course, our overactive imaginations) that brought us to Mrs. Palmaroy. Our friendship continued to grow over the years until we moved on and began our new lives as young adults. Although Mrs. Palmaroy has long since passed, I know that Kevin, Kelli and I will carry a part of her forever in our hearts.